W9-BOL-141

HAIR TWINS

By **Raakhee Mirchandani**

Illustrated by **Holly Hatam**

Little, Brown and Company
New York Boston

Every morning, before I go to school and Papa goes to work, he combs through my waves.

RYE FREE READING ROOM

Gel

He brushes my hair like he does his own, splitting it down the middle, like a river separating two enchanted forests.

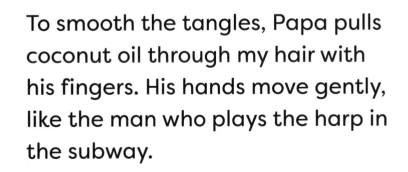

To smooth the tangles, Papa pulls coconut oil through my hair with his fingers. His hands move gently, like the man who plays the harp in the subway.

Sometimes Papa braids my hair, making two twists down the sides of my face.

They remind me of the long,
snowy-white braid my dadi
wears to parties.

When Papa combs his hair, I stand on a stool next to him. I'm almost as tall as he is. I feel like a grown-up.

He calls me his hair assistant.

"Rubber band, please!" he says. I hand him a pink one. Pink is our favorite color.

"Beard brush, please!" he says. I hand him a toothbrush and we both laugh.

Sometimes Papa puts my hair in a bun, tight at the top of my head, like the joora he wears every day.

This is our hair twin look.

"Hair cheers!" I tell him.

When I come home from school, Papa takes my hair down.
I do my special hair dance to shake it out all the way.
He joins me, moving and grooving, wiggling his hips.

"Hip cheers!" I tell him.

Every Friday, to celebrate the weekend, we meet my friends and the grown-ups who love them at the park.

Before we leave, Papa ties his patka, covering his bun. Then he ties his turban, wrapping the fabric around his head. Sometimes he even lets me pick the color!

Papa does my hair one last time for the day.
This is my racing style.

He weaves my hair into one braid, like a
long unicorn tail hanging down my back.

"Can you prance like a unicorn, Papa?"
I ask him, thinking about everyone who
will be waiting for us.

He smiles and lifts me onto his
shoulders.

I know he's ready to race.

Last week we were rocket ships.

Next week we'll be zombies.

Today we all run like unicorns,
a herd tearing through the park.

Braids and buns, spiked and shaved—we all fly together.

My braid taps my back as I soar, and then I smell coconut.

Papa must have caught up to me. I don't even have to look to see his fluffy beard, his warm smile, and his turban.

I know it's him. My hair twin.

Author's Note

Hair Twins is a celebration of the bond between a Sikh father and his daughter, inspired by my husband, Agan, a turban-wearing Sikh American, and our daughter, Satya. As part of their religion, Sikhism, both Agan and Satya don't cut their hair. While Agan and the papa in this book both wear patkas under their turbans, different people have different styles of turban tying.

This story is a window into my family and our tradition, one that started over five hundred years ago in Punjab and that we are proud to maintain and make our own here in America. My hope is that everyone who reads *Hair Twins* feels connected to the relationship between this papa and daughter and inspired to proudly share their own traditions with the world.

© kim lorraine photography

For Agan, patient, adored, and fun.
For Papa, brave, principled, and kind. —RM

To all children and adults who have
ever felt different. —HH

About This Book

The illustrations for this book were done digitally. This book was edited by Samantha Gentry, art directed by Sasha Illingworth, and designed by Neil Swaab. The production was supervised by Patricia Alvarado, and the production editor was Jen Graham. The text was set in Filson Soft, and the display type is Milk & Honey.

Text copyright © 2021 by Raakhee Mirchandani • Illustrations copyright © 2021 by Holly Hatam • Cover illustration copyright © 2021 by Holly Hatam • Cover design by Neil Swaab • Cover copyright © 2021 by Hachette Book Group, Inc. • Hachette Book Group supports the right to free expression and the value of copyright. The purpose of copyright is to encourage writers and artists to produce the creative works that enrich our culture. • The scanning, uploading, and distribution of this book without permission is a theft of the author's intellectual property. If you would like permission to use material from the book (other than for review purposes), please contact permissions@hbgusa.com. Thank you for your support of the author's rights. • Little, Brown and Company • Hachette Book Group • 1290 Avenue of the Americas, New York, NY 10104 • Visit us at LBYR.com • First Edition: May 2021 • Little, Brown and Company is a division of Hachette Book Group, Inc. • The Little, Brown name and logo are trademarks of Hachette Book Group, Inc. • The publisher is not responsible for websites (or their content) that are not owned by the publisher. • Library of Congress Cataloging-in-Publication Data • Names: Mirchandani, Raakhee, author. | Hatam, Holly, illustrator. • Title: Hair twins / by Raakhee Mirchandani ; illustrated by Holly Hatam. • Description: New York : Little, Brown and Company, [2021] | Audience: Ages 4–8 | Summary: Follows a Sikh father and his daughter as they go through their daily hair routine. • Identifiers: LCCN 2019041910 | ISBN 9780316495301 (hardcover) • Subjects: CYAC: Sikh Americans—Fiction. | Fathers and daughters—Fiction. | Hair—Fiction. • Classification: LCC PZ7.1.M6333 Hai 2021 | DDC [E]—dc23 • LC record available at https://lccn.loc.gov/2019041910 • ISBN: 978-0-316-49530-1
PRINTED IN CHINA • 1010 • 10 9 8 7 6 5 4 3 2 1

MIRCHANDANI
Mirchandani, Raakhee.
Hair twins.
03/30/2022

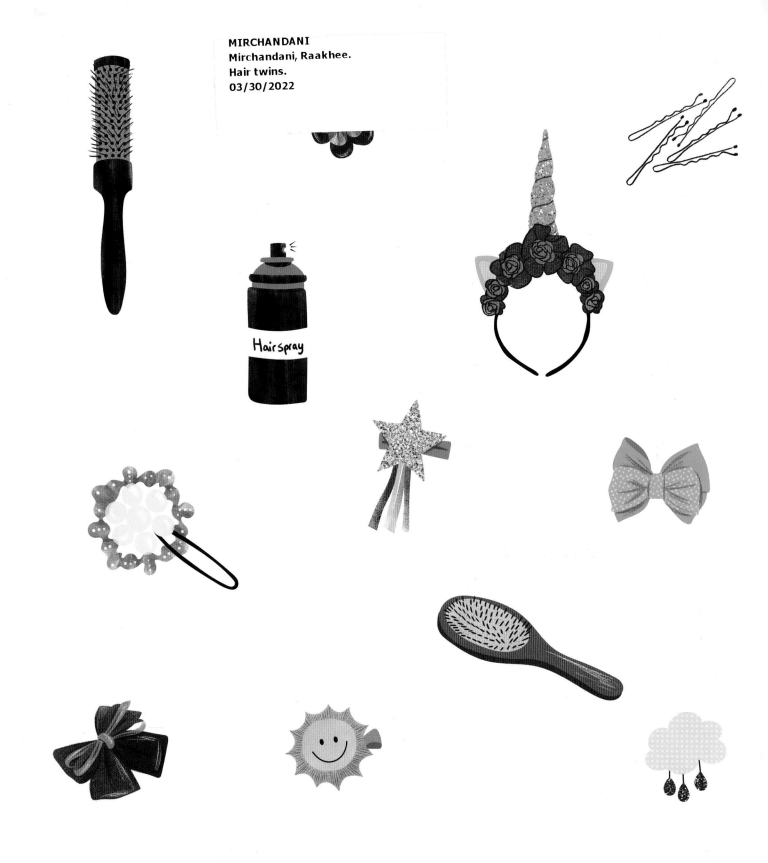